Woodrow Wilson

Lisa Zamosky

Publishing Credits

Historical Consultants
Jeff Burke, M.Ed.
Shannon C. McCutchen

Editors
Wendy Conklin, M.A.
Torrey Maloof

Editorial Director
Emily R. Smith, M.A.Ed.

Editor-in-Chief
Sharon Coan, M.S.Ed.

Creative Director
Lee Aucoin

Illustration Manager
Timothy J. Bradley

Publisher
Rachelle Cracchiolo, M.S.Ed.

Teacher Created Materials
5301 Oceanus Drive
Huntington Beach, CA 92649-1030
http://www.tcmpub.com

ISBN 978-0-7439-0665-4

Table of Contents

Follow the Leader

Very few people are true leaders. Not many people get the chance to be a **university** president. Even fewer citizens get to be governor of a state. And, what are the chances of becoming a United States president? A man named Woodrow Wilson did all these things and more.

Wilson served as president of Princeton University. He was then elected governor of New Jersey. In this role, he made many changes in the state. Then, he became the twenty-eighth president of the United States of America.

While president, Wilson changed the country. He created the Federal Reserve System. This system still exists today. He also set up the first **income tax**. These **economic** (eh-kuh-NAH-mik) systems still help the country today. Wilson also cared about the people. He helped to end child labor. He shortened the work day for laborers. And starting in January 1918, he publicly supported women's right to vote.

Play ball! President Wilson throws out the first pitch on opening day of the baseball season in 1916.

Woodrow Wilson was a professor at Princeton University. Students chose him as the most popular professor. He was the first president who had been a college professor.

The Suffragist Paul

Alice Paul was a firm believer in women's rights. She believed women should have the right to vote. She was a **suffragist** (SUHF-rih-jist) She organized a parade of over 5,000 women. They marched in front of the White House. Paul and her supporters also **picketed** the White House many times.

The League of Nations

Wilson helped form the League of Nations near the end of World War I. Leaders from different countries settled conflicts around the world. Wilson was not able to convince his own country to join the group.

Woodrow Wilson was elected president of the United States twice. He won in 1912 and was reelected in 1916.

Those Early Years

Woodrow is an unusual first name. He was born Thomas Woodrow Wilson. His mother was Jessie Woodrow before she got married. He went by Tommy until after college. Then he started going by the name Woodrow. He thought it sounded more grown up.

Wilson was born in 1856 in Virginia. He had two sisters and one brother. His father was a minister. When Wilson was a young boy, his family moved to Georgia.

A Father's Influence

It was Wilson's father who taught the future president the importance of choosing his words carefully. Discussions with his father helped Wilson learn to be very thoughtful in expressing his ideas. This made him a powerful speaker.

Born in England

Wilson's mother was born in England. This made Wilson the first president since Andrew Jackson to have a parent who was born in another country.

American Civil War

The American Civil War was a war between two regions of the country. The North battled the South. It lasted from April 1861 to April 1865. Wilson lived in the South during the war.

President Wilson's college friends knew him as Tommy Wilson.

Many major battles of the Civil War took place in Virginia, which was where Wilson was born. This image shows the Battle of the Wilderness.

The Civil War began when Wilson was five years old. During the war, some schools were closed. So, Wilson did not have the chance to make many friends his age. He had to learn from his family. They prayed and read the Bible every day. Wilson spent a lot of time with his father. They often walked through town and talked about the things they saw.

Professor Wilson

Wilson went to Princeton University. He then entered the University of Virginia Law School. Next, he went to Johns Hopkins University in Maryland. There, he earned a **doctorate**. He was very well educated.

Wilson had dreams of getting involved in **politics** (PAHL-uh-tiks). He also loved to write. He spent two years writing a book called *Congressional Government*. In it, Wilson pointed out all the things that were wrong with the way **Congress** worked.

Wilson's first teaching job was at Bryn Mawr, a woman's college. Later, he taught at Princeton University. Many other universities wanted him to teach at their schools. But leaders at Princeton talked him into staying. He was soon elected as the president of the university.

Princeton University was called the College of New Jersey when Wilson was a student there.

Wilson and his first wife, Ellen.

Married Man

In June 1885, Wilson married Ellen Axson. She was the daughter of a reverend in Georgia. Wilson saw her at a church service. Wilson went to the reverend's home later that day to visit. Before he left their home that night, Wilson knew he was in love. The Wilsons had three daughters together before she died in 1914.

Ph.D. and a President

Wilson is the first and only United States president to have a doctorate degree.

This book was first published in 1885.

Governor Wilson

While in school, Wilson studied the history of politics. So, it was natural that he would want to become a **politician** (pahl-uh-TIH-shuhn). The people of New Jersey thought he would do a good job. They elected him governor in 1910.

Wilson promised to reform politics in the state. As governor, Wilson proposed many new laws that would change the way things were done. He wanted to see elections run differently. He called for better **benefits** for workers. Wilson wanted lower rates for gas and electricity. He also wanted a special group to take control of the railroads. This group could **regulate** the rates and services.

All of Wilson's changes passed the state congress. His success got him recognized around the country. This set the stage for a higher office.

A Man of His Word

Wilson wanted to be a good governor. When he gave his acceptance speech, he said that he would act independently. This meant that he would not do things based on friendships. He wanted to follow the law and do what was the best for his state.

A Traveling Man

When Wilson became governor of New Jersey, the state did not have an official home for its governor. Wilson continued to live in Princeton with his family. He traveled every day to Trenton, the state capital.

This was Wilson's home in Princeton. It was close to the state capital, Trenton.

Wilson won the election for governor of New Jersey in a landslide. The presidential election would be harder to win.

President Wilson

In 1913, Wilson was sworn in as the twenty-eighth president of the United States. He wanted to help his country. So, he came up with a program called New Freedom. At that time, many children were working instead of going to school. This program changed the child labor laws. It also made jobs safer for adults. The New Freedom program improved conditions for all workers.

When ships brought goods from other places, the shippers had to pay taxes on their goods. This tax was a **tariff** (TAIR-uhf). The tariff made goods expensive for Americans to buy. Wilson asked Congress to reduce tariffs.

These young boys are working in a factory. President Wilson fought hard to get children out of factories and into schools.

This is the Federal Reserve Building in Washington, D.C.

Wilson also helped to set up the Federal Reserve System. This is the central banking system of the United States. Before this time, the United States did not have a strong national bank. A national bank manages a nation's money. The bank makes sure there is enough money to run the country. The Federal Reserve System still exists today.

Income Tax

Wilson set up the first income tax system in the United States. This is a tax that people pay on the money they earn. Income taxes are used by the government to improve the country.

Busy First Lady

Mrs. Wilson had many duties as First Lady. She also had three children to raise. Even so, she found time to help others. Mrs. Wilson wanted to improve the condition of the slums that surrounded the nation's capital. Many residents living there were African Americans. She believed they deserved better living conditions.

The Beginning of War

In 1914, World War I broke out in Europe. It began with an **assassination** (uh-SAS-uh-nay-shuhn). The future king of Austria-Hungary was Archduke Francis Ferdinand. A man killed Ferdinand and his wife, Sophie. Austria-Hungary blamed Serbia (SIR-be-uh). Austria-Hungary and Serbia had been enemies for a while. Countries in Europe took sides. The war placed Germany and Austria-Hungary against France, Great Britain, and Russia.

The *Lusitania* traveled between New York and Liverpool, England. More than 100 Americans died when the ship sank.

Be on My Side!

World War I was a fight between the Central powers and the Allied forces. The Central powers were Germany, Austria-Hungary, and Turkey. The Allied forces were France, Great Britain, Russia, Italy, and Japan.

Did the *Lusitania* Have Weapons?

Many people think that this ship not only carried passengers, but it also had munitions on it. If the ship did have weapons, the British were taking a chance putting passengers on the ship, too.

German submarines were called U-boats. A U-boat, like the one pictured here, fired the shot that sank the *Lusitania*.

In the early part of the war, Germany was not winning the battles on land. So, they looked to their submarines for help. Great Britain's navy stopped ships from going to Germany. These ships had supplies on them. The British navy took the supplies. The British also arrested the German crews. Losing ships like this hurt Germany's war effort. Germany declared the water near Great Britain to be a war zone. The Germans sunk any ship sailing in the waters off the British coast. Most of these ships had **munitions** (myoo-NIH-shunz) that helped Britain's army. Germany had to stop these ships if it wanted to win the war.

In 1915, the Germans sank a British ship called the *Lusitania* (loo-suh-TAY-nee-uh). A total of 1,198 people died. Some Americans were on this ship. This upset President Wilson. Germany did not want the United States to enter the war. So, Germany agreed to stop sinking ships.

Shhh! The Secret Telegram

In spite of its promise, Germany began sinking ships again. Wilson had spent a lot of time **negotiating** (nih-GO-shee-ate-ing) with Germany. He was upset to see this happen and stopped these talks.

Germany knew that sinking ships might bring the United States into the war. So, a German official sent a telegram to Mexico. Telegrams sent during a war had to be top secret. Secret codes were used so no one else could read the messages.

In this telegram, the Germans suggested a plan. When the United States joined the war, Mexico had to help Germany win. That way, Germany would own the United States. If Mexico helped, Germany promised to give the Mexicans land from Texas, New Mexico, and Arizona.

The British **intercepted** (in-tuhr-SEPT-uhd) this telegram. The British even knew how to read the secret code. They shared what they learned with the United States. When President Wilson found out what the telegram said, he was angry. He did not like that Germany was trying to give away parts of the United States. On April 6, 1917, the United States Congress declared war. They supported the Allied forces. This was a turning point in the war.

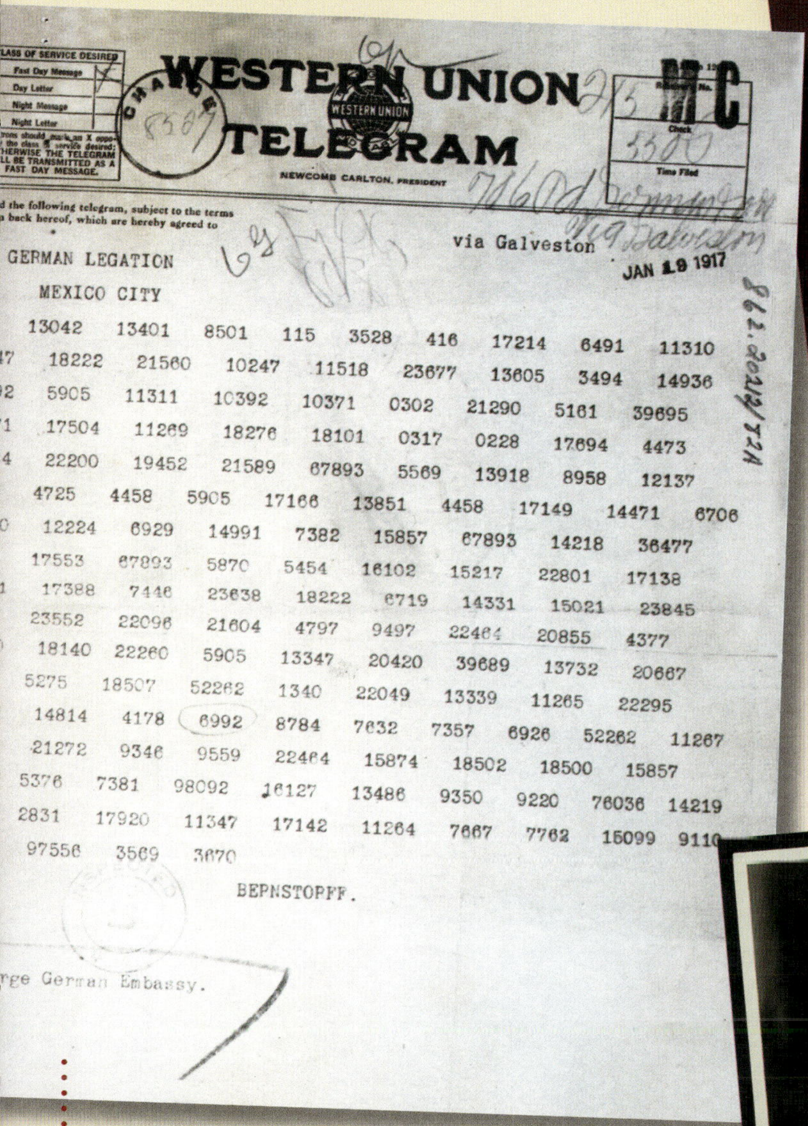
WESTERN UNION
TELEGRAM
NEWCOMB CARLTON, PRESIDENT

d the following telegram, subject to the terms
back hereof, which are hereby agreed to

via Galveston
JAN 19 1917

GERMAN LEGATION
MEXICO CITY

13042 13401 8501 115 3528 416 17214 6491 11310
18222 21560 10247 11518 23677 13605 3494 14936
5905 11311 10392 10371 0302 21290 5161 39695
17504 11269 18276 18101 0317 0228 17694 4473
22200 19452 21589 67893 5569 13918 8958 12137
4725 4458 5905 17166 13851 4458 17149 14471 6706
12224 6929 14991 7382 15857 67893 14218 36477
17553 67893 5870 5454 16102 15217 22801 17138
17388 7446 23638 18222 6719 14331 15021 23845
23552 22096 21604 4797 9497 22464 20855 4377
18140 22260 5905 13347 20420 39689 13732 20667
5275 18507 52262 1340 22049 13339 11265 22295
14814 4178 6992 8784 7632 7357 6926 52262 11267
21272 9346 9559 22464 15874 18502 18500 15857
5376 7381 98092 16127 13486 9350 9220 76036 14219
2831 17920 11347 17142 11264 7667 7762 15099 9110
97556 3569 3670

BERNSTORFF.

rge German Embassy.

The name of the German official who sent this telegram was Arthur Zimmermann. This is why it is called the Zimmermann telegram.

America joined the war not long after Wilson was reelected.

Another Election

In 1916, the public elected Wilson for a second term. During this second campaign, he used the **slogan**: "He Kept Us Out of War!" Most Americans were happy about staying out of the war.

Married Again

Wilson's first wife died during his first term in office. Later, he met Edith Galt. They married while he was running for his second term.

President Wilson and his second wife, Edith

Help Us, America!

In March 1917, the Russian **czar** (ZAR) was overthrown. There were new leaders in Russia. These leaders pulled Russian troops out of the war. Because of this, the Germans moved more troops into France. That gave Germany a better chance of beating both the French and the British. For the Allies to win, they needed the United States to help.

The first thing Wilson did was go to Congress. He gave his most famous speech there. He felt that it was important to have goals when going to war. He thought his plan, called the Fourteen Points, could lead the world to peace in the future.

The last point in his speech was his most famous. He wanted countries to form a League of Nations. When problems happen around the world, this group would help settle them. Wilson believed this group could prevent wars in the future.

The hammer and the sickle represented communism in Russia.

Communism in Russia

After the fall of the czar in Russia, a **Communist** (KAWM-yuh-nist) group took over. The leader of the group was Vladimir Lenin. He knew how hard the war had been on Russia. So, the Communists withdrew from the war immediately.

Calling All Men!

On April 6, 1917, Congress passed the declaration of war. A draft system was created. This system called 2.5 million men for military service.

Czar Nicholas II of Russia was overthrown during the Russian Revolution.

During his presidency, Wilson suffered from a stroke. Some people believe that it was a result of his endless campaigning in support of the League of Nations.

President Wilson addresses Congress.

This picture shows the "Big Four" seated at Versailles. These leaders were from Italy, Great Britain, France, and the United States of America.

Fourteen Big Points

After the United States entered the war, it did not take long for a **truce**. The Germans wanted to end the war. This happened on November 11, 1918. The leaders of all the countries met in Paris, France. Wilson attended this peace **conference** (KON-fuhr-entz) to end the war. On June 28, 1919, a peace treaty was finally signed.

Wilson presented his Fourteen Points plan to other world leaders. Five of the points talked about preserving peace in the world. Eight points had to do with land and territories. He also told them about his final point, the League of Nations.

The other world leaders were not sure of Wilson's plan. Great Britain wanted more land to **colonize** (KAHL-uh-nize). France wanted revenge for their destroyed land. Wilson's Fourteen Points did not fit in with the ideas and plans of other countries.

The Treaty of Versailles (vuhr-SI) was signed by Germany and the Allies. Many of Wilson's points were not accepted. But other leaders did accept his idea of a League of Nations.

This is the United Nations headquarters in New York City.

Nobel Peace Prize Winner!

Woodrow Wilson won the 1919 Nobel Peace Prize for his hard work to establish the League of Nations.

League of Nations

In the end, the League of Nations was not able to prevent wars from happening. Following World War II, the organization became the United Nations. The United Nations still works toward world peace today.

Celebrating Veterans

Veterans Day is celebrated on November 11 every year. This holiday honors the men and women who fought in America's wars. The date of this holiday is a reminder of the **armistice** that ended World War I. It was signed at 11:00 A.M., November 11, 1918.

The First Female President?

Edith Wilson took messages into the president's bedroom when he was sick. Then, she came out with answers to those messages. Some historians call her the first female president. They say she was really running the country. Mrs. Wilson took care of her husband from the time of his stroke until his death.

Warnings from His Doctor

When told by his doctor that he should stay home and rest, Wilson said, "I do not want to do anything foolhardy, but the League of Nations is now in its crisis, and if it fails, I hate to think what will happen to the world . . . I cannot put my personal safety, my health, in the balance against my duty."

Keeping a Secret from the Public

Wilson knew he had to get the United States to join the League of Nations. The United States was now a world leader. They had to be a good example to other countries.

But many Americans **opposed** Wilson's plan. Some people felt it would create too many problems for the United States. The United States had problems of its own. Americans did not need to meddle in the problems of other countries.

By this time, Wilson was 60 years old. Against his doctor's advice, Wilson traveled around the United States. He gave speeches about the League of Nations. While on this long tour, Wilson suffered a stroke. His doctor and wife hid his condition from the public. He finished his term in office. He lived for three more years. Wilson died in 1924.

The United States never did join the League of Nations. But after World War II, American leaders understood what Wilson had been saying all along. Nations had to work together to keep peace. The United States joined the United Nations. Wilson's ideas have lived on to help bring peace.

After leaving the White House, Wilson still supported important causes. Here, he is giving money to support medical research.

President Wilson on one of his last speaking tours. He was promoting the League of Nations.

Other World Leaders

Woodrow Wilson was an important leader during the early 1900s. There were other leaders at the time who also helped change the world. The following pages describe these leaders.

The Kaiser of Germany

Wilhelm II was the kaiser (KI-zuhr), or emperor, of Germany. He was a fighter with a quick temper. He felt it was important to have a strong army and navy. He could not sit by and let Britain's Royal Navy be the best in the world. Wilhelm wanted a war, and he wanted to be well prepared for it.

Wilhelm saw his chance when the assassination of Archduke Ferdinand took place. He pushed Austria-Hungary to take revenge. He told them his country would fight with them. The Austrians listened to him. And, the war started.

Not long after the United States forces joined the war, Germany gave up. Wilhelm left Germany and lived the rest of his life in **exile** (EK-sile) in Holland.

Wilhelm II led Germany into a world war.

Queen Victoria reigned from 1837 to 1901. This time period is often called the Victorian Era.

All in the Family

Wilhelm's grandmother was the queen of England until 1901. He claimed he never would have fought Great Britain if she were still in power. Wilhelm was also the cousin of Russia's czar, Nicholas II.

He Didn't Realize

Some wonder if Wilhelm knew that pushing Austria-Hungary to take revenge on Serbia would bring others into the war. France, Russia, and Great Britain all joined the war against Germany and Austria-Hungary. Wilhelm tried to pull back once he realized what he had done. But, by then it was too late.

This part of the world was at the heart of World War I.

Czar Nicholas II
of Russia

Who Was Vladimir Lenin?

Vladimir Lenin was the leader of the 1917 Russian Revolution. He felt that everyone should have equal money, land, and food. This idea led to a communist government in Russia.

Trying to Kill the Czar

Lenin's brother was killed in 1887 for planning to kill the czar. After his brother's death, Lenin became a full-time **revolutionary** (rev-uh-LOO-shuhn-air-ee).

Other World Leaders (cont.)

The Last Czar of Russia

The Romanov (row-MAW-nawf) family had ruled in Russia for three centuries. But by 1917, Czar Nicholas II was out of touch with the common people. He had no idea how they struggled to survive. He married a German princess. The Germans were the enemy, so some did not like that he married a German. Nicholas also put his trust in a Russian monk named Rasputin (ras-PYOO-tuhn). This made his **advisors** angry. They thought Rasputin gave Nicholas bad advice.

Russia had fought a war against Japan that ended in 1905. The country was not prepared to fight another strong enemy. The people had not recovered from the first war yet. The Russian people wanted out of World War I.

A man named Vladimir Lenin (VLAH-duh-mir LEH-nuhn) had been away from Russia for a long timc. Thc Russian government did not like Lenin's ideas. Germany's Kaiser Wilhelm II sent Lenin back to Russia. Wilhelm hoped that Lenin would start a rebellion. Lenin led the Russian Revolution and set up a new government.

Lenin was kicked out of school for his radical ideas. These ideas helped him to become the leader of the Russian Revolution.

Other World Leaders *(cont.)*

Monarch Franz Joseph

Franz Joseph was the ruler of Austria-Hungary. Hungary wanted to be independent of Austria. Joseph married a woman named Elisabeth. The Hungarians thought of her as their monarch. The two of them shared the power and ran the large country together.

Joseph had no living **heirs** (AIRZ). His nephew was Archduke Francis Ferdinand. Ferdinand would be the next king in Austria-Hungary. But, the archduke was killed on a trip to Serbia. Within three weeks of his assassination, Joseph wrote a harsh letter to Serbia.

He gave Serbia only two days to reply. They agreed to almost all of Joseph's demands. It did not matter, Joseph was looking for a reason to make war. He soon declared war on Serbia, and World War I began.

Franz Joseph I, leader of Austria-Hungary

Archduke Francis Ferdinand, his wife Sophie, and two of their children

Disliking His Successor

Joseph did not care much for his nephew, Ferdinand. Joseph did not like Ferdinand's wife either. So, he refused to attend their wedding. After the assassination, he did not even attend Ferdinand's funeral.

A Long Reign

Joseph died in 1916 after 68 years of power! He knew at the end of his life that his country would not win the war.

Some leaders do better jobs at leading than others. Good leaders take their time to think through the decisions they have to make. They stand up for what they believe. Sometimes, it is hard to tell which leaders are most effective. But history always sorts out the real leaders from those who claim to be.

Glossary

advisors—people who give advice and guidance to a leader

armistice—a temporary end of fighting through agreement among parties; a truce

assassination—to murder by surprise attack; usually a prominent person for political reasons

benefits—special employee payments through money, insurance policies, or public assistance programs

colonize—to take control over land in other parts of the world and send people to live there and rule

Communist—someone who believes in an economic idea that lets the government distribute land and goods

conference—a meeting

Congress—the national lawmaking body of the United States, consisting of the Senate and the House of Representatives.

czar—rulers or emperors of Russia long ago

doctorate—a higher-education degree; a Ph.D.

economic—having to do with money

exile—forced absence from a homeland

heirs—people who are next in line to rule a country

income tax—tax imposed on the money citizens earn at their jobs

intercepted—stopped something before it got to its destination

munitions—weapons including bullets, guns, and gun powder for making bombs

negotiating—talking out problems and coming to a resolution

opposed—went against something

picketed—marched in protest holding signs

politician—a person who is in politics or in government service

politics—having to do with government offices

regulate—to bring order to something

revolutionary—someone who wants to overthrow one government and replace it with another

slogan—a saying

suffragist—a person who supports extending the right to vote to others, especially women

tariff—a price placed on goods by a government

truce—a temporary end of fighting by agreement of the opposing sides of a war; an armistice

university—a school that people can attend after high school

Index

Image Credits

cover The Library of Congress; p.1 The Library of Congress; p.4 The Library of Congress; p.5 (top) Photos.com; p.5 (bottom) The Library of Congress; p.6 The Library of Congress; p.7 The Library of Congress; p.8 The Library of Congress; p.9 (left) The Library of Congress; p.9 (right) Dover Publications, Inc.; p.10 The Library of Congress; p.11 Corbis; p.12 The Library of Congress; p.13 Photos.com; p.14 The Library of Congress; p.15 Corbis; p.16 Corbis; p.17 (left) The National Archives; p.17 (right) The Library of Congress; p.18 Lena Lir/Shutterstock, Inc.; p.19 (top) A. A. Pasetti; p.19 (bottom left) The Library of Congress; p.19 (bottom right) Bettmann/Corbis; p.20 The Granger Collection, New York; p.21 Christopher Walker/Shutterstock, Inc.; p.22 The Library of Congress; p.23 (top) The Library of Congress; p.23 (bottom) Bettmann/Corbis; p.24 The Library of Congress; p.25 (top) The Library of Congress; p.25 (bottom) Teacher Created Materials; p.26 The Library of Congress; p.27 Photos.com; p.28 The Granger Collection, New York; p.29 The Granger Collection, New York